LAP

Go. **READ!**™

These levels are meant only to guide you
you and your child can best choose a book that's right.

Level 1: Kindergarten–Grade 1 . . . Ages 4–6
- word bank to highlight new words
- consistent placement of text to promote readability
- easy words and phrases
- simple sentences build to make simple stories
- art and design help new readers decode text

Level 2: Grade 1 . . . Ages 6–7
- word bank to highlight new words
- rhyming texts introduced
- more difficult words, but vocabulary is still limited
- longer sentences and longer stories
- designed for easy readability

Level 3: Grade 2 . . . Ages 7–8
- richer vocabulary of up to 200 different words
- varied sentence structure
- high-interest stories with longer plots
- designed to promote independent reading

Level 4: Grades 3 and up . . . Ages 8 and up
- richer vocabulary of more than 300 different words
- short chapters, multiple stories, or poems
- more complex plots for the newly independent reader
- emphasis on reading for meaning

For Johnny, with love and laughter

LEVEL 4

2 4 6 8 10 9 7 5 3 1

Published by Sterling Publishing Co., Inc.
387 Park Avenue South, New York, NY 10016
Text © 2008 by Deborah Zemke
Illustrations © 2008 by Deborah Zemke
Distributed in Canada by Sterling Publishing
c/o Canadian Manda Group, 165 Dufferin Street,
Toronto, Ontario, Canada M6K 3H6
Distributed in the United Kingdom by GMC Distribution Services,
Castle Place, 166 High Street, Lewes, East Sussex, England BN7 1XU
Distributed in Australia by Capricorn Link (Australia) Pty. Ltd.
P.O. Box 704, Windsor, NSW 2756, Australia

I'm Going To Read is a trademark of Sterling Publishing Co., Inc.

Library of Congress Cataloging-in-Publication Data

Zemke, Deborah.
  Don't bargain with the tooth fairy : 44 ridiculous rules every kid should know /
written and illustrated by Deborah Zemke.
     p. cm.—(I'm going to read)
  ISBN-13: 978-1-4027-5547-7 (alk. paper)
  ISBN-10: 1-4027-5547-3 (alk. paper)
  1. Conduct of life—Juvenile humor. I. Title.

PN6231.C6142Z45 2008
818'.5402—dc22

2007029927

Sterling ISBN-13: 978-1-4027-5547-7
ISBN-10: 1-4027-5547-3

For information about custom editions, special sales, premium and
corporate purchases, please contact Sterling Special Sales
Department at 800-805-5489 or specialsales@sterlingpub.com.

I'm Going To READ!™

DON'T BARGAIN WITH THE TOOTH FAIRY!

44 Ridiculous Rules Every Kid Should Know

by Deborah Zemke

STERLING
New York / London
www.sterlingpublishing.com/kids

INTRODUCTION

You have to follow rules everywhere—in school, at home, even in the supermarket. Wherever you are, it's important that everybody follow the rules because you know what happens when someone doesn't.
You know what happens when your class doesn't line up quietly for recess and twenty-four screaming kids all try to get out at the same time.

Still, it's hard work to follow all the rules all the time. So just for fun here are some rules that are so silly you will never need to follow them—just read them and laugh!

CHAPTER 1
AT HOME

1 Don't leave your stuff all over the house. Instead, put it in a big pile in the middle of the living room. That way you'll know where everything is.

2 Never try to hide an elephant
under your bed.

3 Keep your homework in a safe place.

4 Don't sit too close to the TV.

If your breath fogs the screen,
you are sitting too close.

5 Use the right tool for the job.

Use a rake to
clear the table.

Use a sprinkler
to wash the dishes.

Dry the dishes
with a hair dryer.

6 Do not bargain with the tooth fairy.

The tooth fairy always wins.

7 Don't snorkel in the bathtub.
You never know who you'll run into.

8 Don't play hockey on the dining room table.

9 Never try to brush your teeth and your hair at the same time.

10 Keep your room clean by throwing everything in the closet.

11 Don't play electric guitar in the car,

in the shower

or before 6 a.m.

12 Don't skateboard down the stairs.

13 Don't leave any science experiment in the refrigerator for longer than six months.

14 Don't watch more than seventeen
hours of television in one day—
even if it's Saturday.

15 Do not paint your face or your
room with your mom's makeup.

16 Make your bed every day. Here's how:

Stand at the foot of the bed. Gently lift the bed up until your pillows, sheets, blanket, comforter and secret stash of chewing gum slide neatly into place. Lower the bed.

CHAPTER 2
IN PUBLIC

17 Always obey the speed limit
in the supermarket.

18 Do not ask Mr. Pobblestone
what he swallowed.

19 Do not ask Mrs. Pobblestone
what she swallowed.

20 Always tie your shoelaces,
but not together.

21 What to say when an adult asks, "How old are you?"

Correct answer:

"I'm 8 years, 10 months, 2 weeks, 4 days, 6 hours, 27 minutes and 16 seconds old."

Wrong answer:

"I'm 8. How old are you?"

22 Do not blow your nose in your socks.

23 Never interrupt unless you're really about to burst.

24 Don't climb telephone poles,
flagpoles, or tadpoles.

25 Don't stare at anyone strange.

26 Be cheerful, even when
your home run has just gone
through Mrs. Garcia's window.

27 Never wear anyone else's underwear.

28 Don't practice juggling at the store.

29 What to say when an adult asks,
"What do you want to be when you grow up?"

Good answers:

    rocket scientist, brain surgeon, really rich

Not such good answers:

    lizard, bank robber, professional wrestler

CHAPTER 3
IN SCHOOL

30 When your teacher asks if there are any questions, do not raise your hand and ask, "What time is recess?"

31 Don't chew on your pencil.
The eraser tastes better.

32 Don't do loop-de-loops on the swings.

33 Do not call your teacher an old bat unless
she is hanging upside down from the ceiling.

34 Learn how to sit still. Practice this until you can sit perfectly motionless for hours, even after the bell has rung and everyone else has gone home.

35 Bring the teacher lots of presents.

GOOD PRESENTS:

apple

coffee mug

pencil with her name on it

flowers from your garden

NOT SUCH GOOD PRESENTS:

yesterday's bologna sandwich

crushed soda can

chewed-up pencil with her name on it

poison ivy

36 Don't make sudden stops when you're at the front of the line.

37 Do not practice your penmanship
by writing notes to your friends.

38 Don't dress like the class clown even if you are one.

39 Don't dress like the teacher's pet—especially if the teacher likes gerbils.

40 What to say when an adult asks, "What did you learn in school today?"

The A+ answer: "5+3=8"

The F- answer: "What school?"

41 Don't lose your lunch money.
You need it to buy candy bars.

42 Be helpful.
Offer to keep the class
tarantula in your desk.

43 There isn't a teacher on this planet who will accept the excuse that your dog ate your homework, so don't try to feed your homework to Spot, Fido, Fluffy, or any other family pet.

44 Study these rules every day.
You never know when
they'll be on the test.